The Tug-of-War

An African Tale
Retold by Julie Ellis
Illustrated by Meredith Thomas

Chapter 1

Tortoise Is Angry

Tortoise was angry. He had been talking to Elephant and Hippo, and they had both been very rude to him.

Elephant had said, "You are so small."

Hippo had said, "You are so slow."

"I may be small and slow," said Tortoise, "but I am clever. They will be sorry they were rude to me."

Tortoise sat and thought for a few days. At last he thought of a really good trick to play on Elephant and Hippo.

Chapter 2

Tortoise Has a Plan

Tortoise went to visit Elephant. Elephant was sleeping under a big tree.

"Wake up, Elephant," yelled Tortoise. "I want to talk to you."

Elephant woke up. He was upset with Tortoise.

"What do you want?" he asked.

"I'm here to challenge you to a tug-of-war," answered Tortoise. "I may be small, but I am very strong."

Elephant laughed.

"I accept your challenge," he said.

"I know what will happen,"
thought Elephant. "One tug on
the rope, and Tortoise will fly over
the trees, never to be seen again."

Tortoise arranged to meet Elephant at
sunrise the next day in the tall grass
between the trees and the river.

Then Tortoise went to visit Hippo. Hippo was lying in the cool water.

"Hippo," yelled Tortoise. "I want to talk to you."

Hippo lifted up his head. He was upset with Tortoise.

"What do you want?" he asked.

"I'm here to challenge you to a tug-of-war," answered Tortoise. "I may be slow, but I am very strong."

Hippo laughed.

"I accept your challenge," he said.

"I know what will happen," thought Hippo. "One tug on the rope, and Tortoise will fly into the water, never to be seen again."

Tortoise arranged to meet Hippo at sunrise the next day in the tall grass between the trees and the river.

Tortoise was very busy that night. He made a very long and very strong rope. He put the rope in a long line stretching from the edge of the trees, through the tall grass, to the edge of the river.

Then he hid himself in the tall grass, halfway between the trees and the river.

At sunrise, Elephant woke up. He saw one end of the rope lying in the grass near the trees.

At the same time, Hippo woke up. He saw the other end of the rope lying in the grass near the river.

"Tie the rope around your middle!" cried Tortoise. "When I say go, we will start our tug-of-war."

9

Chapter 3

The Tug-of-War

Elephant and Hippo both did as Tortoise said. They couldn't see Tortoise, and they couldn't see each other because of the tall grass.

"Ready . . . set . . . go!" called Tortoise.

Elephant pulled with all his might.

Hippo pulled with all his might.

"Tortoise is strong," thought Elephant, "but not as strong as I am," and he pulled harder.

"Tortoise is strong," thought Hippo, "but not as strong as I am," and he pulled harder, too.

Elephant and Hippo pulled and pulled. They wouldn't stop because they each thought they were pulling Tortoise.

Tortoise hid in the grass and watched them. When he thought they had had enough, he cut the rope with a sharp stick.

There was a loud splash from one end. Hippo had fallen into the water. There was a loud crash from the other end. Elephant had bumped into a tree.

Both Hippo and Elephant were too exhausted to move

The next day Tortoise went to see Elephant, who was standing under a tree too exhausted to move.

"I'm sorry I was rude to you, Tortoise," said Elephant. "You may be small, but you are very strong."

Then Tortoise went to see Hippo, who was lying on the river bank too exhausted to move.

"I'm sorry I was rude to you, Tortoise," said Hippo. "I will not be rude to you ever again."

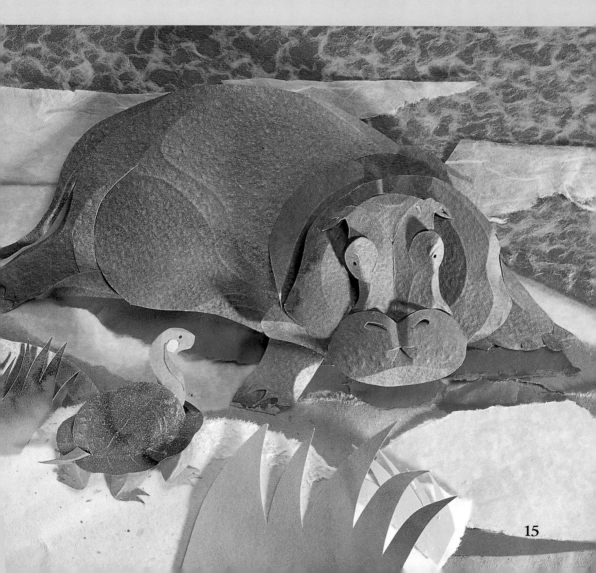

Tortoise smiled happily to himself.

"I may be small and slow, but I'm also quite clever."